First published 2014 by Macmillan Children's Books
a division of Macmillan Publishers Limited
20 New Wharf Road, London N1 9RR
Basingstoke and Oxford. Associated companies throughout the world
www.panmacmillan.com
ISBN: 978-0-230-77285-4 (HB)
ISBN: 978-1-4472-4327-4 (PB)
Text and illustrations copyright © Chloë and Mick Inkpen 2014
1 3 5 7 9 8 6 4 2
A CIP catalogue record for this book is available from the British Library.
Printed in China

Zoe and Beans

Chloë & Mick Inkpen

Pirate Treasure!

MACMILLAN CHILDREN'S BOOKS

'Let's build our sandcastle here,' said Zoe.

'Perfect!' said Oscar.

'Woof!' said Beans.

Oscar's baby sister
said nothing.

Zoe grabbed her spade
and started digging.
Soon there was sand
flying in all directions.

'Here's your spade, Evie,' said Oscar.
But Evie wasn't listening.
She had found an interesting thing.
It was round and shiny.

'Evie's found some treasure!'
said Oscar.
'It must be pirate treasure!
Everyone dig!'

But there was no treasure.
Just a **great big** hole.

'Perhaps the treasure is at the bottom of the **sea!**' said Zoe. So they blew up the blow-up crocodile and looked in all the rock pools.

Every rock pool seemed to be full of shiny, glistening things...

... but none of them
was treasure.

'What about that island!'
said Oscar.
'A pirate would hide his treasure
on an island!'

But the island was
smaller than it looked.
'There's nowhere to
hide treasure here,'
said Zoe.

'There must be treasure in a cave!'
said Zoe.
'You could hide **loads** of treasure
in there!'

The cave was scary.
Dark and scary.
'Hold my hand Evie,' said Oscar.
'Don't let go!'

'I think I've found something!'
said Zoe. 'It's round!
And a bit shiny!

It must be the **treasure!**'

But all they found
was a bottle top . . .

. . . and an old flip-flop.

Zoe was disappointed.
And a bit grumpy too.
So was Oscar.
'We're **never** going
to find the treasure.'

Beans wasn't grumpy.
He was wagging his tail
  and sniffing Evie's pocket.
'Stop it Beans!' said Zoe.
  But Beans didn't stop.
He kept on sniffing at
  the gold coin.

Suddenly he was off!

'He can smell the **treasure!**' said Oscar.

'He's going to sniff it out!'

Sniff sniff
along the beach . . .

sniff sniff
over the rocks . . .

sniff sniff
up the steps . . .

sniff sniff along the sea wall . . .

sniff sniff . . .

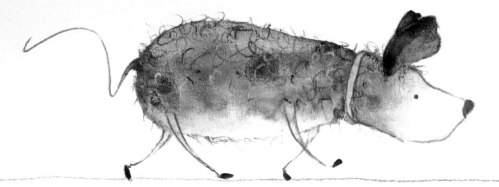

...there's the **treasure!**

Yum!